EARDISLEY SCHOOL LIBRARY

For my wife Malgosia

First published in Great Britain in 1989.
Burns & Oates Ltd.,
Wellwood, North Farm Road,
Tunbridge Wells, Kent, TN2 3DR.

Originally published in Germany under the title
Thomas und die Taube by Patmos Verlag, Düsseldorf

Original edition © Patmos Verlag 1987

English Translation © Burns & Oates Ltd, 1989

ISBN 0 86012 177 1

Typeset by Scribe Design, Gillingham, Kent
Printed in Spain by Salingraf S.A.L. Bilbao

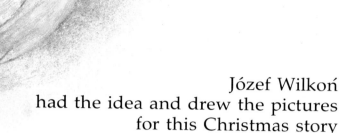

Józef Wilkoń
had the idea and drew the pictures
for this Christmas story

Rudolf Otto Wiemer
wrote the original text

Michael Walsh and Rosalind Dace
translated it into English

Thomas
and the Dove

BURNS & OATES

A biting cold wind had blown for many days.
It swirled round the trees and stripped the branches bare
of the last few autumn leaves.
Dark snow clouds hung low in the heavens.

Then the snow fell. It snowed and snowed.
Huge white flakes whirled down, covering the dark
earth and thick woolly fleece of the sheep with an icy
winter blanket.

It was goodbye to the long sunny autumn and to the
happy days spent out in the fields.
'It is a good thing my dove is almost finished', said
Thomas, and he held up a bird carved out of wood.
'The only thing left to do is to paint it white. Do you like
my beautiful dove?' he asked his dog.
But the dog only yawned, and blinked sleepily.
Why should Thomas be asking him to admire a dove
carved out of wood, when they were just about to set
out on a journey?

Thomas led his large flock over the snowy hills towards the village.

The sheep crowded together to keep warm, and bleated and butted along behind the young shepherd boy and his dog.

They longed to reach the warm stable at their journey's end.

Before leaving, Thomas had painted his beautiful dove completely white. Now he held it tightly in his hand.

He was going to look after his precious little dove, which gleamed pure white like the crisp newly-fallen snow.

It was the middle of the night before they reached the village. The cold was just beginning to bite at Thomas's nose, creeping right through to his finger-tips.

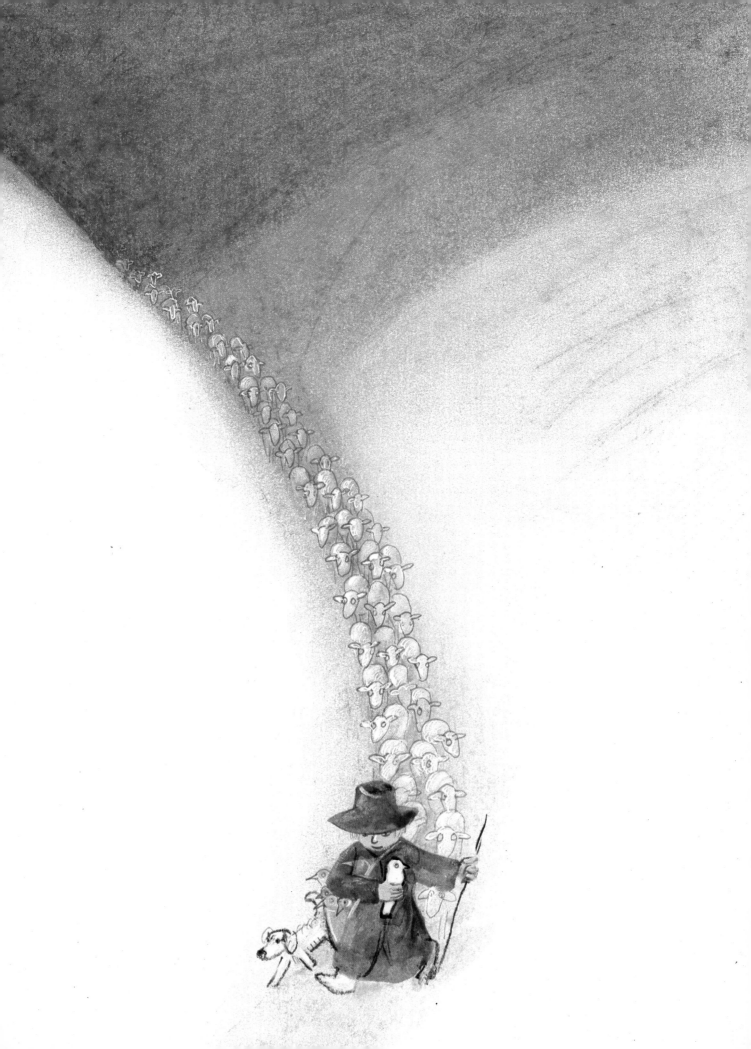

As Thomas entered the village he saw a
large crowd of people gazing up at the sky.
There was great excitement.
'What's the matter?' asked Thomas.
'Don't you know what has happened?',
they said.
'Just look at the star!'.

Thomas rubbed his eyes and looked up. In
the heavens a beautiful star was shining, a
star brighter than Thomas had ever seen
before.

'What is it?' he asked.
'It is the star of Bethlehem', the villagers
replied.
'Jesus is born! That's where we are all going
now.
We are going to see the Christ-child to offer
him presents.'
And they laughed and shouted out for
sheer joy.

The following morning Thomas fed the sheep.
His dog was happy because he was given a great big
bone.
Then the young shepherd boy went to visit the farmer
who owned the sheep.
'Hello' said the farmer.
'Why have you left my sheep unguarded?'
'I would love to go and see Jesus with the other
villagers', Thomas answered, 'and I would like to give
him a present.'
'What sort of present?' asked the farmer.
'My little white dove', said Thomas.
The farmer laughed. 'Go on then. But wouldn't it be
better to give Jesus a little white lamb? That would please
him even more.'
'Oh no', said Thomas, as he quietly stroked his wooden
bird.
'My dove is very beautiful, and I love it so.'

Meanwhile, the other villagers were already making
their way along the road to Bethlehem.
Amongst them were farmers and shepherds, as well as
rich people whose horses and donkeys were carrying
their belongings, and expensive gifts of gold, precious
stones, velvet and silk.
Thomas ran along the road as fast as he could, anxious
to catch up with them.
The beautiful bright star shone down from above,
showing him the way.

As Thomas caught up with the crowd of
people they turned round and looked at the
little shepherd boy.
He saw they were all laughing at him.
He showed them his little dove: 'Isn't it
beautiful?' he said 'This is my present for
Jesus.
Don't you think it will make him happy?
I carved and painted this dove myself.'
The villagers laughed.
'What?' they replied. 'A wooden dove for
a King?
Haven't you anything better?
No gold? No money?
Not even a sheep or a little lamb?'
They laughed even more as they made fun
of him.

Then the crowd started to move forward again, full of excitement at the thought of seeing Jesus.
Thomas was sad. He slowly stumbled along behind them.
'Perhaps they are right,' he thought. 'Their gifts are much more valuable than my little carved dove.'
Feeling very disheartened he gently held the dove in his hand. His heart felt heavy, and as he walked along the road he became even sadder.

Tired of hearing the people laughing and making
fun of him, Thomas ran past them all, right up to
the front of the procession.

There he saw an old man on a donkey. He went up
to him.
'Hello,' said Thomas, 'Have you got a present for
Jesus?'
'Yes,' replied the old man.
'I am going to give him my donkey. Of all the things
that I own, my donkey is the most valuable, and
the one I love best.'
'But what will you do without your donkey?' asked
Thomas.
'Well, I shall just have to make do,' said the old
man.
'I am sure Jesus will need the donkey more than I.
Are you taking a present to him as well?'

Thomas showed the old man his dove.
'Do you think he will like it just a little bit?'
'Of course he will', replied the old man. 'It is such
a beautiful white dove! I am sure Jesus will love it
as much as you do. Just take it to him and see.'
The old man's words made Thomas feel very
happy.

The road stretched out before them as they
marched on and on, through deep dark
valleys and wild glens, up hill and down
dale.
Thomas began to feel tired and weary.
He could hardly keep his eyes open, and
he occasionally stumbled over his own feet.
But all the time he kept tight hold of the
little dove in his hand.
The old man noticed Thomas falling. He
turned and said,
'Why don't you sit on my donkey and ride
for some of the way. I can walk alongside
for a while.'
He lifted the shepherd boy up on to the
donkey's back and called out 'Gee-up!'
The donkey twitched his ears and began to
trot briskly along with his lighter load.

At long last they reached the end of their journey. There, beneath the great bright star they saw a stable.

And in the crib was Jesus lying on a bed of straw and hay, wrapped in swaddling clothes.

The people forgot the long journey and their tiredness. They pressed forward, kneeling before him offering their gifts, each more beautiful than the last; expensive gifts, many of them made out of gold and precious stones.

Jesus did not laugh or cry. He looked at the gifts without a sound.

And because he was only a baby, the people handed their gifts to his father Joseph and to his mother Mary.

At last it was Thomas's turn.
Shyly he stepped forward and showed
Jesus his little white dove.
As Thomas watched, Jesus began to smile.
Then he stretched out his hands to take the
dove, laughing with joy.

Holding his breath, Thomas stepped right up to the crib.
The people also held their breath.
This just could not be! They could not believe what they
were seeing.
Thomas gently placed the little wooden dove in the
baby's hands.
For a moment Jesus held the dove.
Then he gently opened his hands.
And the bird spread out its wings.
As Thomas watched he felt happier than he had ever felt
before. His little dove was alive! The bird flew out of the
baby's hands and soared upwards, higher and higher
towards the great bright star, graceful, living and white.